Disney
The Little Mermaid

Ladybird Books

Ariel the mermaid was the youngest daughter of Triton, king of the merpeople. Ariel and her friend Flounder the fish were always getting into trouble with King Triton.

First edition

Published by Ladybird Books Ltd Loughborough Leicestershire UK

© 1991 THE WALT DISNEY COMPANY
Printed in England (7)

One day, Ariel promised her father that she would sing in a special concert, but she forgot all about it. Instead, she and Flounder went searching for human treasure in a shipwreck.

King Triton was furious. He thought humans were dangerous, and he told Ariel to stay away from them.

But Ariel disobeyed her father. The very next day she swam up to the surface to look at a ship.

On board was a handsome young prince called Eric. It was his birthday and the crew had just given him a birthday present – a statue of himself.

Suddenly, a terrible storm blew up. The crew jumped to safety in the lifeboat, but Prince Eric went back to save his dog, Max. The ship was wrecked and Eric was thrown into the sea.

The little mermaid dived towards the prince and pulled him to the shore.

Ariel's friend Scuttle the seagull told her that Eric was dead, but Ariel didn't believe him. She sang softly to Eric and slowly he began to open his eyes. Before the prince could see her clearly, Ariel leapt back into the sea with a splash. All Eric could remember was her beautiful voice.

Ariel had fallen in love with the handsome young prince, but she knew that Eric would never marry a mermaid. "If only I had legs," she thought sadly.

When King Triton found out that Ariel was in love with Eric he was so angry that he destroyed her collection of human things – even the statue of the prince that Flounder had saved from the wreck.

Now, King Triton had one great enemy –
Ursula the sea witch. Ursula wanted to rule
Triton's kingdom, and when she heard about
the family quarrel, she saw her chance.

Ursula sent her servants, Flotsam and Jetsam, to see Ariel. "Ursula can help you," they said. "She can make your dreams come true. You and your prince can be together forever."

In exchange for Ariel's voice, Ursula agreed to turn Ariel into a human – but only for three days.

"If," said Ursula, "Prince Eric hasn't kissed you by sunset on the third day, you'll become a mermaid again and be in my power forever."

Ursula held up a contract for Ariel to sign.

"Do we have a deal?" asked Ursula.

"Yes," said Ariel.

Ursula then chanted a complicated spell… and the little mermaid became human.

The next thing Ariel knew, she was up on the beach. And she had legs!

Suddenly, Prince Eric appeared in the distance. He was walking with Max, thinking about the girl with the beautiful voice who had rescued him.

When he saw Ariel he was convinced that *she* was the one who had saved him. But when he found out that Ariel couldn't speak, he decided that he must be mistaken.

Still, Eric found Ariel enchanting, and they spent every minute of the next two days together. Ariel was sure that Eric was falling in love with her, but not once did he try to kiss her.

Ursula began to worry that Ariel would succeed in winning Eric's heart. On the third day, she turned herself into a beautiful girl and went to meet Eric.

Round her neck she wore a little shell in which Ariel's voice was trapped. When Eric heard Ursula speak with Ariel's voice, he fell under her wicked spell. Eric asked Ursula to marry him that very evening.

Feeling very pleased with herself, Ursula boarded Eric's ship to get ready for the wedding. But Scuttle, spying on Ursula through a porthole, saw her true reflection in the mirror.

"It's the sea witch!" he thought. "I must stop the wedding!" And he flew off to tell Ariel.

That evening, Scuttle returned to the ship with his friends from the seashore. They swooped down and tugged at Ursula's hair, clothes and necklace. The shell holding Ariel's voice fell onto the deck. It shattered, and the voice inside floated back to its rightful owner.

"Eric!" cried Ariel.

"It's you!" exclaimed Eric. "You're the one who saved me!"

But before Eric could take Ariel into his arms to kiss her, the sun sank below the horizon and Ariel turned back into a mermaid. Ursula, no longer in disguise, grabbed Ariel and dragged her beneath the waves.

When Triton heard what had happened he went to Ursula and begged her to free his daughter.

"A deal's a deal," said Ursula, waving the contract in his face. "Unless you take her place, Ariel is mine forever!"

Triton had no choice. He handed over his crown and trident. Cackling with glee, Ursula used the trident to turn Triton into a small slimy creature, wriggling on the sea bed.

Ariel was in despair. But Eric came to her rescue, flinging a harpoon at Ursula.

The sea witch was furious! She began to swell, turning the sea into a roaring whirlpool.

An ancient shipwreck was thrown up from the sea bed by the giant waves and Eric leapt aboard. He went straight for Ursula, crushing her beneath the ship's bow.

The trident Ursula had been holding sank down to the sea bed. Triton touched it and became king once more.

Triton now realised how much
Ariel loved the handsome
young prince. He knew
that she would never be
truly happy living in his
ocean kingdom. Though
he knew he would miss
her terribly, he turned
her back into a
human.